For Jo, Emma, Rob and Hussein,
who make any day feel like Christmas! – MS

For Nancy xx – EE

Bloomsbury Publishing, London, Oxford, New York, New Delhi and Sydney

First published in Great Britain in 2017 by Bloomsbury Publishing Plc
50 Bedford Square, London WC1B 3DP

www.bloomsbury.com

BLOOMSBURY is a registered trademark of Bloomsbury Publishing Plc

A CIP catalogue record of this book is available from the British Library

ISBN 978 1 4088 7107 2 (HB)
ISBN 978 1 4088 7108 9 (PB)
ISBN 978 1 4088 7106 5 (eBook)

All papers used by Bloomsbury Publishing are natural, recyclable products made
from wood grown in well managed forests. The manufacturing processes
conform to the environmental regulations of the country of origin

Printed in China by Leo Paper Products, Heshan, Guangdong

1 3 5 7 9 10 8 6 4 2

How Many QUACKS till Christmas?

Mark Sperring

Ed Eaves

BLOOMSBURY

LONDON OXFORD NEW YORK NEW DELHI SYDNEY

It's very nearly Christmas
on this here Merry Farm
and lots of farmyard creatures
are trying to keep CALM.

"How many **oinks** till Christmas?"
the piglets SQUEAL with glee.

"How many **oinks** till Christmas?
Will Santa visit me?"

"How many **baas** till Christmas?"
The lambs skip high and low.

"How many **baas** till Christmas?
Do we have *long* to go?"

"How many **neighs** till Christmas?"
the foals all ask their mum.

"How many **neighs** till Christmas?
Is the waiting *nearly* done?"

"How many **quacks** till Christmas?"
the ducks all want to know.

"How many **quacks** till Christmas?
And – **QUACK!** – will there be snow?"

"How many **moos** till Christmas?"
the calves want to be told.

"How many **moos** till Christmas?

And **BRRRRRR** it's getting cold!"

"How many **woofs** till Christmas?"
asks one excited little pup.

"How many **woofs** till Christmas?
Can I hang my stocking up?"

Then, just as snowflakes flutter down,
eyes flutter fast asleep.

And stay that way till morning
when they're woken with a . . .

CHEEP!

"How many **cheeps** till Christmas?"
whispers Cockerel's little son.
"How many **cheeps** till Christmas, Daddy?
Is it more than one?"

"Well," grins Daddy Cockerel,
"I've good news for ALL of you . . ."

"There are NO MORE **cheeps** till Christmas . . ."

"Just a cock-a-doodle-do!"

And with jolly **OINKS** and happy **NEIGHS**, the big day's – **QUACK QUACK** – here!

So . . . "Merry Christmas, EVERYONE!"

the whole farm WOOFS and CHEERS!